For my dad, son, nieces, and sister.

And in memory of my mother, Shirley; Annie; AV; Ruby;
and all the makers who have inspired me.

GLOSSARY

ôhô / owl / oh-HOE

pimihâwipîsim / migrating moon / pimmyHOW-PEEsim

ayîkipîsim / frog moon / EYEyicky-PEEsim

Text and illustrations copyright © 2019 by Julie Flett

First published in the U.K. in 2020

19 20 21 22 23 5 4 3 2 1

Greystone Kids / Greystone Books Ltd.
greystonebooks.com

Cataloguing data available from Library and Archives Canada
ISBN 978-1-77164-473-0 (print)
ISBN 978-1-77164-474-7 (epub)
ISBN 978-1-77164-475-4 (epub)

FSC
www.fsc.org

MIX
Paper from
responsible sources
FSC® C012700

Editing by Kallie George
Copy editing by Paula Ayer
Jacket and interior design by Sara Gillingham Studio
Jacket illustration by Julie Flett
The illustrations in this book were rendered in pastel and pencil, composited digitally.

Printed and bound in Malaysia on ancient-forest-friendly paper by Tien Wah Press

Greystone Books gratefully acknowledges the Musqueam, Squamish, and Tsleil-Waututh peoples on whose land our office is located.

Greystone Books thanks the Canada Council for the Arts, the British Columbia Arts Council, the Province of British Columbia through the Book Publishing Tax Credit, and the Government of Canada for supporting our publishing activities.

Canada

Canada Council
for the Arts
Conseil des arts
du Canada

BRITISH
COLUMBIA

BRITISH COLUMBIA
ARTS COUNCIL
An agency of the Province of British Columbia

Birdsong

Julie Flett

GREYSTONE KIDS

GREYSTONE BOOKS • VANCOUVER/BERKELEY

Spring

It's a mucky spring morning as we pack up the last of our belongings and leave our little home in the city by the sea.

I'm going to miss my friends and cousins and aunties and uncles. I'm going to miss my bedroom window and the tree outside.

"Goodbye, tree friend," I whisper.

We drive through the country and over the mountains,
alongside rivers and fields of horses.
We stop to see a lone coyote crossing the road.

Our new home sits on a hill overlooking a field,
and past it, another home. In that home
lives an older woman named Agnes.
The field is covered in snowdrops.

Our new home has
two trees outside . . .

. . . and creaky stairs inside.

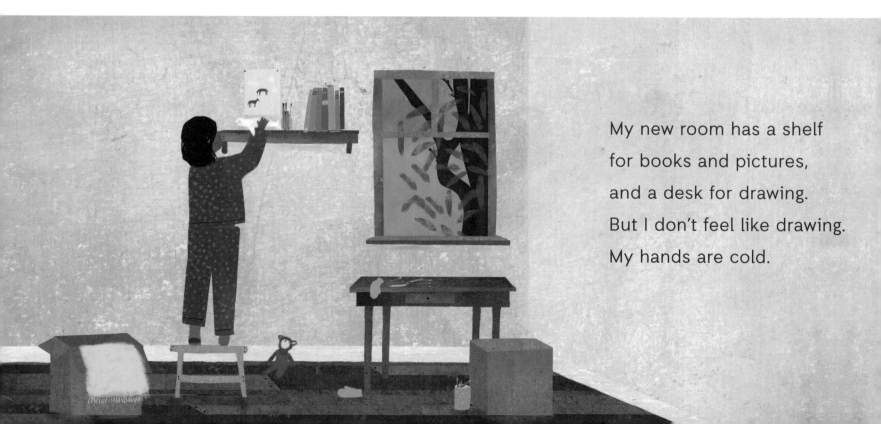

My new room has a shelf
for books and pictures,
and a desk for drawing.
But I don't feel like drawing.
My hands are cold.

My mom and I bundle up together under the covers
in our new home in the country, far from the sea.

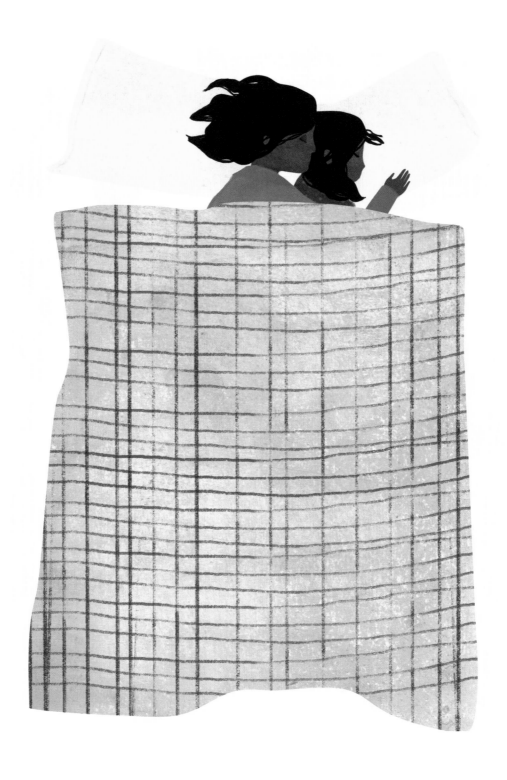

Summer

Our new home hums with peeps
and whistles and ribbits and chirps.

I watch Agnes, our neighbor,
working on something in her yard.

"Why don't you visit her, Katherena?"
my mom says.

I nod. "Okay."

I take our dog, Ôhô, with me.
Ôhô means owl in Cree.

"Hello, Agnes?" I say.

"You must be Katherena!" she says.

Woooof! Ôhô barks.

"Your mom has told me all about you,"
Agnes says. "She says you love to draw."

"I do."

Agnes loves to make things out of clay.

She shows us around her yard.

There are berries and flowers and

so many of her clay things.

They look like the branches and birds and flowers.

"Visit me again soon, Katherena!"
Agnes says with a smile.

I smile back and give her a big wave.

I can't wait to go home and start drawing.

Fall

I do visit Agnes again—

and again

and again.

Agnes digs in her garden.
I help by gathering extra leaves
that'll get mixed into the soil.
The worms love this.

It's getting cold and windy and creaky.
Agnes says she's getting creaky too.

"Would you like to see what I'm
working on, Katherena?" she asks.

"I'd like that," I say.

Agnes is working on a pot that's round and bright.
She tells me about waxing and waning moons.
I tell her about Cree seasons. This month is called
pimihâwipîsim—the migrating moon.

Here comes the moon and two shiny seagulls.

And there go the geese.

Winter

It's Ôhô's first snow.
We toboggan until my snowsuit is soggy
and Ôhô is covered in tiny snowballs.

After, we warm up with Mom by the fire
and then help her finish making
salmon stew to share with Agnes.

Agnes hasn't been out as much
and needs a little help over the winter.
She likes the salmon stew.
Her daughter, who has come to
stay for a while, likes it too.

Agnes sends me home with a cup full of bulbs—
snowdrop bulbs to plant in the field next autumn.
They look like tiny moons.
They give me more ideas for pictures.

My fingers itch in my mittens.

Spring

Agnes has grown weaker over the winter.
Still, from her bed, we can hear
the spring birds singing their songs.
And the tickle of the branches against her window.

We listen to the sounds together.

The snowdrops are peeking out.
I wish Agnes could see them.

I have an idea!

I run home and gather up all my drawings.

Agnes's daughter meets me at the door,
and we take two ladders from the closet.

When we're done, Agnes says it's like a poem for her heart.

Then I sit with Agnes and talk about making things:
mucky things and things with string and song
and paper and words. And then we sit quietly together,
on Agnes's bed, until it's time to say goodbye.

I leave with an ache in my heart,
but I'm so glad to know my friend Agnes.

"Hello, Mom. Hello, Ôhô. Hello, home, with two trees and creaky stairs."

Later that night, ayîkipîsim, the frog moon, is full.
My mom and I bundle up together in our home.

My hands feel warm and the covers feel soft,
and I think of my friend until I fall asleep.